Dedicated to Finn and Scout.
You are brave, strong, kind, and
smart. Your father and I love you
as high as airplanes fly.

My Dad, The Pilot

My dad is a pilot, so I'm unique,

he leaves for the skies and adventure each week.

Some days he's home, and some days he's not,

but nothing can change the bond that we've got.

If you ask me where he's at, sometimes I don't know.

Maybe chilly Fairbanks or sunny Cabo.

It's different every day; it's constantly changing,

our schedule is crazy and always rearranging.

Nothing can get in the way of our love,

not even miles of sky up above.

Love isn't ever bothered by distance,

it's felt far away and very persistent.

There are times I get sad when he can't tell me goodnight,

but I know soon enough he'll be holding me tight.

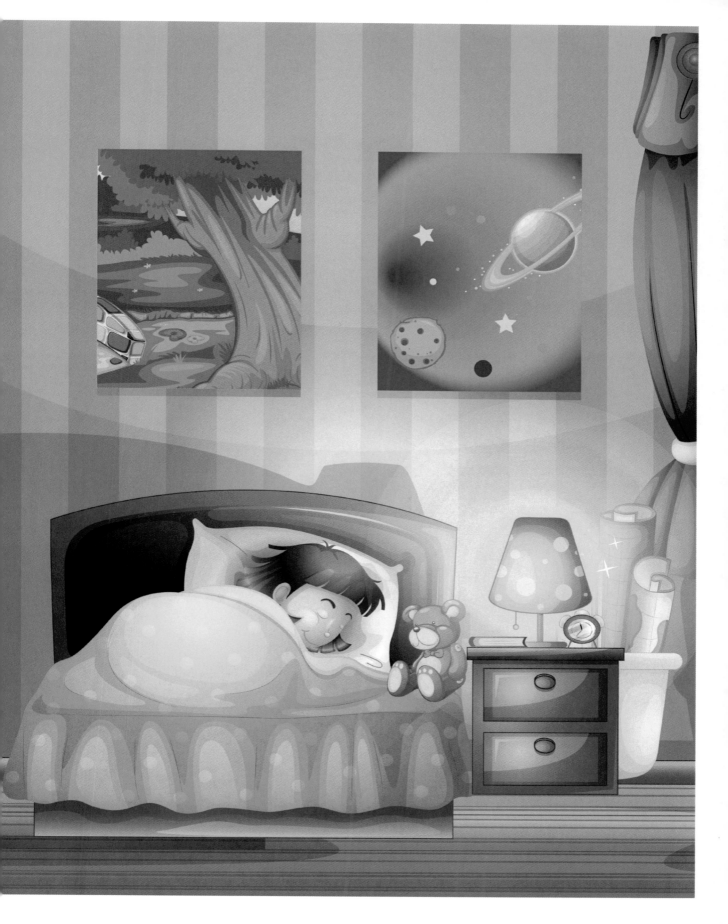

While he's up in the air, he has precious cargo,
he's looking out for the people In tow.

He flies passengers from place to place,

he takes care of them all and gets them home safe.

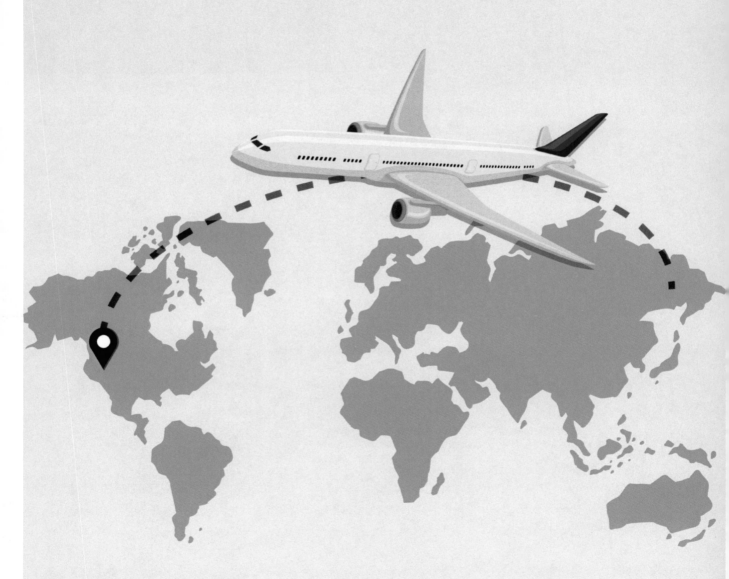

When he's at work, he takes care of us too;

he provides a good life for me and for you.

When I tell him goodbye, I'm brave, and I'm strong,

for I know he'll be back and it won't be long.

"Till we're hugging his neck, and holding him tight,

and asking, 'hey dad, how was your flight?'"

Our family is different I guess you could say,

our family loves in a special way.

Our love is so big; it's over the moon,

because we love a pilot that's coming home soon!